MAD
LOOK
AT THE
FUTURE

Written by **Lou Silverstone**

Illustrated by **Jack Rickard**

Edited by **Nick Meglin**

WARNER BOOKS

A Warner Communications Company

For Mary and Matt,
In hope
that the Future
will be as Mad
as the past...
L.S.

WARNER BOOKS EDITION

**Copyright © 1978 by Lou Silverstone,
Jack Rickard and E. C. Publications, Inc.**

ISBN 0-446-88174-0

Title "MAD" used with permission of its owner,
E. C. Publications, Inc.

**This Warner Books Edition is published by
arrangement with E. C. Publications, Inc.**

Warner Books, Inc., 75 Rockefeller Plaza, New York, N.Y. 10019

Ⓦ A Warner Communications Company

Printed in the United States of America
Not Associated with Warner Press, Inc. of Anderson, Indiana

First Printing: May, 1978

10 9 8 7 6 5 4 3 2 1

CONTENTS

FUTURE "COMEDY / HORROR" MOVIES

"Young Dracula"
(or "Blazing Blood")

Count, I'll bet you have never seen your reflection in a mirror!

How did you know that?

And have you ever been photographed?

Yes, but the pictures never came out! In my year book, there's a blank space where my picture belongs! It says, Sydney Dracula: Cheer Leader 4, Student Council, Senior Play, Hall Patrol, but **no picture!**

Of course! Because, my friend, you are a **vampire!** We just have to awaken the dormant Dracula blood and you'll be **one of us!!**

SEVERAL MONTHS LATER

He's got it, by George, he's got it! Count, it's time for you to **solo!**

Orlock was right! This beats the credits and debits life of a **boring accountant!**

SEVERAL MONTHS LATER

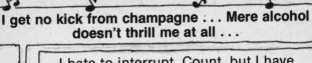

A FORTNIGHT LATER

SEVERAL MONTHS LATER.

FUTURE IMPROVEMENTS

That Will Effect Our Everyday Lives

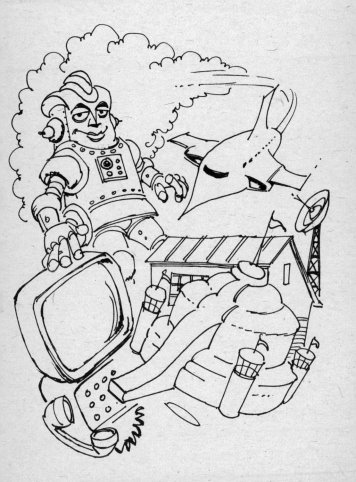

FUTURE OFFICE EQUIPMENT—Computerized dictating and typing machines will make secretaries obsolete!

FUTURE STADIUM—Will be entirely enclosed, air-conditioned, every seat will have an excellent view and a TV screen to see instant replays! Everything will be perfect—except the players!

FUTURE TELEPHONES—You'll be able to see the person you're talking to!

FUTURE SCHOOLS—Will replace teachers with computers and television techniques!

FUTURE HEATING—Will be done by solar energy from the sun! It will be cheaper, cleaner and more efficient!

FUTURE AIRPLANES—Will cross the ocean in less than an hour!

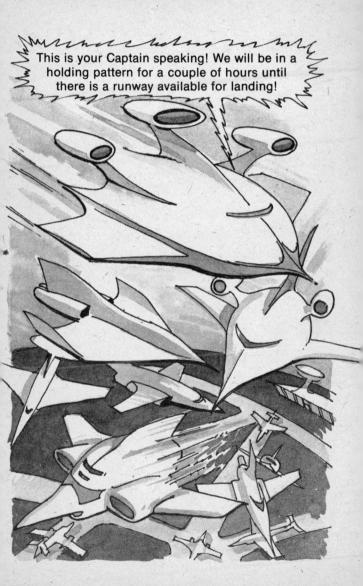

FUTURE BOOKS

What's so "future" about the Hardy-Har Boys? They've been around forever, and they're still going strong! Which means that they'll still be around whenever, getting involved in adventures like . . .

The HARDY-HAR BOYS in...

The Mystery of the Mysterious Missing Ship

CHAPTER I

THE SCREAM

Fenwick Hardy Har, the internationally famous investigator, gazed proudly at his two sons, the dark-haired, serious Woe and the fair-haired, exuberant Fink. Hardy Har had reason to be proud of his husky teenage boys because if it weren't for their uncanny ability as detectives, Fenwick would be still pounding a beat in the Bronx. Sometimes, however, he worried about the muscular Fink and the well-built Woe. There was no sibling rivalry between them, they never had fights or argued or swore or read girlie books or looked dirty words up in the dictionary or played doctor like other boys and girls their age. "Well," thought Fenwick, "as long as they keep solving all my cases, who cares!"

Plump, good-natured Shet Moron, the boys' best friend, entered the Hardy Har living room. "Hi," he greeted good-naturedly.

"Hello, plump, good-natured Shet," chided Mrs. Hardy Har, the boys' slim, attractive Mother, "would you like to stay for supper? We're having tapioca pudding, strawberry shortcake and apple pandowdy!"

"What's for dessert?" salivated the stout Shet.

Before Mrs. Hardy Har could reply, they heard the sound of breaking glass followed by a loud frightened scream!!

'What's For Dessert?'

CHAPTER 2

THE MYSTERIOUS STRANGER IN THE BATHTUB

"Eureka", exclaimed Woe, "it's Aunt Intrude!"

The youthful detectives bounded up the stairs. They were met at the top of the stairs by their frightened Aunt Intrude, Fenwick Hardy Har's tall, angular, unmarried sister. "There's a m—m—m—man in my bathtub," she gasped in a terrified voice, then slumped unconscious to the floor.

Fink and Woe raced into the bathroom and tore aside the shower curtain. Aunt Intrude hadn't imagined it! There *was* a mysterious man in her bathtub!

There Was A Mysterious Man In The Tub.

CHAPTER 3

ANOTHER SCREAM

"Who are you?" cried Woe angrily.

"What are you doing in our Aunt Intrude's bathtub?" blurted out Fink.

"At the moment I'm getting wet," chuckled the tall, trench-coat clad stranger. Then his voice became serious, "I'm Agent Grim of the CIA," he said grimly. "I'm afraid I fell through your skylight, I came here to see the Hardy Har boys on a matter of grave national importance."

"We're the Hardy Har boys," said Woe.

"You won't find us in the bathtub except on Saturday night," grinned Fink exuberantly.

Suddenly another shrill scream resounded through the house.

"Gloryosky," cried Woe, "it's Mother!"

'I'm Agent Grim Of The C.I.A.'

CHAPTER 4

KIDNAPPED

Fink and ·Woe, followed by the dripping Agent Grim darted from the bathroom, leaped over the unconscious body of their unmarried, tall aunt and bounded down the stairs. Aunt Intrude opened her eyes, saw Agent Grim chasing after the boys and ·fainted again. The boys raced past the panting, chubby, Shet, who was arriving at the top of the stairs.

"Gosh," he gasped, "I just got here and everybody's going the other way!" The Hardy Har boys found their frightened, slender Mother in the living room.

"Mother, what's wrong?" blurted out Fink.

"It's your father . . ." she sobbed.

"Gee, Mom, you know how Dad is," sighed Woe, "Sometimes he gets a little romantic, but that's no reason to scream."

"No, you don't understand! Your father's been kidnapped," came her anguished cry.

'I Just Got Here, And Everybody's Going The Other Way.'

CHAPTER 5

THE WARNING

"Kidnapped!" echoed Fink and Woe.

"I found this," exclaimed Mrs. Hardy Har, handing Woe a torn scrap of paper. It read . . .

> WARNING TO THE HARDY HAR BOYS—
> ROSES ARE RED
> VIOLETS ARE BLUE
> WE'VE GOT YOUR OLD MAN AND
> WE'RE GOING TO GET YOU TWO TOO!

"What does it mean?" inquired Fink in a puzzled voice.

"I think I can explain," offered Agent Grim. "An American ship disappeared and we have reason to believe it was seized by an unfriendly country. Acting on our intelligence reports, a battalion of marines were dispatched to the island where we believed the ship was being held."

"I guess that will show *that* unfriendly country not to mess with the good old U.S. of A," interrupted Fink.

Agent Grim flushed and continued, "Unfortunately, our intelligence proved to be false. The marines invaded the wrong island and were captured. Your assignment, should you choose to accept, will be to land on the island and rescue the Marines!"

'The Marines Invaded The Wrong Island.'

CHAPTER 6

THE STRANGE COINCIDENCE

"But what does this have to do with my husband's mysterious kidnapping?" inquired Mrs. Hardy Har anxiously.

"By a strange coincidence Mr. Hardy Har was kidnapped by the same people who are holding the Marines prisoners." explained Agent Grim earnestly.

"You're probably right," agreed Fink. "*All* of our adventures are filled with strange coincidences like that!" Suddenly there was a deafening roar as if a boulder was crashing down the stairs!

A Heavy Weight Came Crashing Down The Stairs.

CHAPTER 7

PERMISSION GRANTED

The loud, crashing sound turned out to be the chubby Shet, who had fallen down the stairs. "Hi," he grinned sheepishly, "I tripped over your Aunt Intrude. Nothing like a trip to stimulate the old appetite!"

Woe and Fink quickly filled Shet in on the missing ship, the captured marines and their kidnapped father, as Shet filled in on cookies and milk.

"Just another normal day at the Hardy Har house," smiled Shet eatingly.

"Well, boys, what do you say?" inquired Agent Grim. "It could be dangerous. You could be captured, held prisoner and tortured!"

"It sounds like keen fun", replied Woe. "Can we help the CIA, Mother?" Before the slender Mrs. Hardy Har could reply, Aunt Intrude appeared and said in a shaky voice, "Don't let them go, they might get hurt. Why don't you send them to summer camp instead? They could make me a wallet or pot holder!"

Calm, sensible, tall, slim, attractive Mrs. Hardy Har had faith in her strong, muscular sons' ability to cope with danger. "You can go if you promise to be careful and to brush your teeth every night," she said sensibly.

"Can I go too?" pleaded Shet.

Agent Grim grinned grimly. "Okay, Shet, you're on the rescue team. Now, let's get moving. There's a car outside to take you to the airport."

'You Could Be Captured, Held Prisoner And Tortured.'

CHAPTER 8

GERONIMO!

The next morning aboard a government plane, Shet, Fink and Woe winged their way across the ocean. Woe opened an envelope marked SECRET ORDERS. He and Fink studiously studied the instructions and maps. "These guys are really thorough," admired Woe. "While we sneak onto *one* side of the island, the Navy is going to bomb the *other* side as a diversionary tactic."

Suddenly they heard a muffled cry, "HELP".

"It's Shet," cried Fink, attempting to leap to his feet. He had forgotten about his seat belt. The young investigators unsnapped their seat belts and raced to the end of the plane from where the cries were originated.

"It's coming from here," said Woe, pointing to a small door marked LAVATORY. Fink and Woe thrust themselves against the door. It did not yield! They pushed harder and finally the door burst open!

"Gee," grinned Shet, "don't you guys ever knock before entering the john?"

"You had us worried," snapped Woe.

"How do you think I felt, being stuck in here. I might have missed lunch," chuckled Shet.

"Now hear this!" came a voice over the loud speaker. "Adjust your parachutes and prepare to jump!"

'Don't You Guys Ever Knock?'

CHAPTER 9

ABANDON RAFT

The three parachutes floated lazily toward the choppy blue ocean. The young sleuths and their overweight best friend landed in the sparkling, azure water. They quickly inflated their raft and started rowing in the direction of the island. "There's one thing that has me puzzled," blurted Shet in a puzzled voice. "We're going to rescue the Marines, but what about the missing ship and its' crew?"

"According to Agent Grim, the ship was released before the Marines landed," explained Woe.

"Then why send in the leathernecks?" inquired Shet.

"In order to teach the world that you can't fool with the USA." snapped Fink.

Suddenly there was a strange hissing sound.

"What's that?" wondered Fink.

"I hope it's not a sea serpent," gulped Shet.

"It's worse than that!" declared Woe soberly. "We've sprung a leak!"

'We've Sprung A Leak!'

CHAPTER 10

INTO THE SEA

Woe squinted and peered into the distance. "Look," he exclaimed excitedly, "it's the island. We'll have to swim for it."

The teenage investigators and their chubby chum took off their shoes, rolled up their trousers and slid overside into the choppy water. They were all strong swimmers and soon neared the island. Suddenly from the other side of the island came the sound of exploding shells. The sky was filled with the rocket's red glare and bombs bursting in air, which gave proof in the night that the Navy was there.

"It's the Navy, right on schedule," grinned Fink.

They scrambled up the sandy beach and plunged into the dense underbrush. "According to our maps, the prison compound should be straight ahead," reported Woe.

"Here's a barbed wire fence," announced Woe.

"Luckily we brought our wire cutters," exclaimed Fink as he cut through the fence.

Suddenly Shet cried out, "Fink, Woe, look!!"

They Were All Strong Swimmers.

CHAPTER 11

TO THE RESCUE

"It's the Marines", gasped Shet, "The United States Marines." Unable to contain himself, Shet broke into a chorus of the Marine Hymn. The teenaged detectives and their over-weight singing classmate found themselves surrounded by a group of puzzled Marines.

"We're the Hardy Har boys," explained Woe. "We're here to rescue you."

"We've heard of you fellows," replied a tall Marine Sgt. "We *figured* something was up when we heard the shelling."

"That's the Navy using a diversionary tactic," offered Woe.

"Incidentally," smiled the Marine Sgt., "My name is Kelly, this is Cohen and Vermicelli".

"Gosh," laughed Fink, "we *never* had names like that in any of our books before. And one of you is even *black*. Not that we *noticed*, mind you!"

The black marine grinned, his white teeth flashing, "I'm Thompson," he said as he burst into song, "The Cohens and the Kellys, . . . the Thompsons and Vermicellis . . . . . They're all part of this tenement symphony . . .."

"It's really true," blurted Shet," you guys do have rhythm."

"We have a rendezvous with a sub at 0700," declared Woe, studying his watch. "We'd best get a move on."

"But where's Dad?" exclaimed Fink.

'We're Here To Rescue You.'

CHAPTER 12

CASE CLOSED

On board the sub, Fink and Woe were amazed to be greeted by their famous investigator father, Fenwick Hardy Har. "Dad," exclaimed Woe in a bewildered voice, "how did you get here? We thought you were kidnapped."

"That's right," grinned Mr. Hardy Har, "I was kidnapped by the MAFIA."

A swarthy faced man in a pin striped suit grunted in a horse whisper, "We snatched him as our patriotic duty."

Noticing the young detectives puzzled expression, Agent Grim laughed and explained, "We had your Dad kidnapped in order to insure your helping us with the rescue mission."

"Wow!" declared Woe admiringly. "You CIA guys think of everything!"

"We try to," declared Agent Grim. "I think it's safe to say, thanks to the efforts of the CIA, the country finds itself in the shape it's in today."

"Where's Shet?" inquired Mr. Hardy Har.

"I'll bet I know," grinned Fink. "He's wherever the *food* is!"

"That's right," came Shet's voice. "I'm stuck in the galley and please don't rescue me!"

His remark drew forth peals of laughter.

THE END

'I'm Stuck In The Galley.'

FUTURE TALK SHOWS

Have you seen talk shows lately? They're running out of *big name* celebrities who want to risk their fame and fortune by bombing out before a national audience! And they're using up *small name* celebrities at a rate that will diminish the supply in the not-so-distant future! So what will they do? Well, there's always *no name* celebrities . . .

Hi, folks! Welcome to the MERV GRINNING SHOW!

We have a delightful show for you tonight. I'd like you to meet our first **guest!** He's currently working as the checkout clerk of the **All-Night Supermarket!** One of the great names in grocery, Mr. Price and Pride himself, **Wally Lumpkin . . .**

My next guest doesn't need any introduction so I won't introduce him . . . haha! Seriously, one of the great names in **insurance,** winner of 4 Golden Policies for selling a **million** dollars worth of insurance, the talented, Norman Edelstein . . .
Thanks, Merv, it's a pleasure to be on the show.

FUTURE NEWSPAPER ARTICLES

MADTROPLIS—It has been reported by a reliable source that the following chapter in this book concerns itself with what the title of this chapter says it does. And since redundancy is an art in the hands of those looking to fill space and not say anything, we now present a chapter containing examples of future newspaper articles . . .

FRANCE AWARDS CROIX DE GUERRE TO TERRORIST

French Prime Minister honors terrorist.

PARIS—Abdula ben Abdula, a member of the Black November Liberation Army, was given Frances' highest honor, the Croix de Guerre, in a ceremony in Paris today. Abdula, who blew up a plane load of civilians at Orly Airport, outside Paris, is the first Arab to receive the prestigious medal.

The French Prime Minister denied there was anything politically involved in the presentation and claimed it was a coincidence that a new oil deal was signed with OPEC. He angrily told reporters, "The honor of France cannot be bought!"

THE YANKEES SIGN ALL STAR TEAM

Yankee owner and his newest employees

NEW YORK—The baseball world was shocked today when the Yankees announced that they had signed nine members of the National League All Star team to long term contracts. The Yankees denied that they are trying to "buy a World Series."

The Yankee owner was quoted as saying, "I got these guys for only a billion dollars and I just can't resist a bargain!"

The Yankees also announced an increase in ticket prices. Box seats will cost fifty dollars; reserved seats, thirty-five dollars; general admission, twenty-five dollars and the bleacher seats, all ten of them, remain at $1.75.

STREISAND TO STAR IN NEW KONG FLICK

Barbra meets her latest co-star

HOLLYWOOD—Warner Studios announced that they are going to make the most expensive movie in history; a musical version of King Kong starring Barbra Streisand. Filming is due to start next month if it's convenient with the singing star. In addition to the starring role, Ms Streisand will produce, direct and design Kong's wardrobe. Her name will appear above the title and in larger letters than King Kong, because as the actress said, "I'm a bigger star!"

LAKERS SIGN 14 YEAR OLD TO MULTI-MILLION CONTRACT

The new Los Angeles Lakers star works out under the watchful eye of the Coach.

LOS ANGELES—The Lakers have solved their long quest for a "big man" with the signing of Matthew 'Bigfoot' Dink, the eight foot star of the Orange Julius Erving Grammar School.

The 200 college recruiters who have been camping in 'Bigfoot's' backyard for 2 years claim the Lakers are exploiting the youngster and depriving him of a chance for a good education.

Dink was at the bank and unavailable for comment.

AUTO MAKERS GIVEN TEN YEARS TO DEVELOP ANTI-POLLUTION CAR

CONGRESS WARNS AUTO MAKERS

WASH., D.C.—A pollution free car moved a step closer to reality today when the House Committee on Environmental Control warned the car manufacturers to stop pussyfooting around and come up with a workable anti-pollution device within ten years.

The auto lobby protested that this wasn't nearly enough time, but said they would *try* to meet the latest deadline.

The Committee agreed with the auto lobby that the cost for research and development of the anti-pollution device should be passed on to the car-buying public. "They want cars, they want clean air—they want everything! Why *shouldn't* they pay for it!" a spokesman said.

BANKRUPTCY FOR FUN CITY?

MAYOR DENIES CITY IS GOING BROKE

Mayor talking to reporters

NEW YORK—In an impromptu press conference outside City Hall, the Mayor denied the rumor that New York City will run out of funds by next Tuesday. The mayor said, "I give you my word, we will not be bankrupt on Tuesday, no matter what you heard. And you can quote me." When asked about the possibility of going bankrupt on Wednesday, the Mayor replied, "No comment."

RED GALS CRUSH U S MEN IN OLYMPIC SWIM

Victory Ceremony

MOSCOW—Russian and East German women swimmers scored a complete sweep in today's competition. For the first time in Olympic history, the American men failed to win a single swimming medal as the talented red ladies splashed their way to victory.

Mark Spitz, the American Coach, saw all his Olympic records broken. He told reporters, "They're just too big and strong for our guys! They're also too big and strong for the Russian guys!"

OIL SPILL RUINS ENTIRE SEABOARD

Liberian Tanker Aground

NEW JERSEY—The Liberian super-tanker, The Rusty Schlock, came apart today when it smashed into the rocks at Ambrose Lighthouse off Sandy Hook. The Coast Guard watched helplessly as billions of gallons of crude black oil poured into the ocean. The Coast Guard said that the gigantic spill will close every beach from Maine to Florida.

The Shill Oil Co., owner of the crippled tanker, advised the public not to be alarmed. Despite the loss of oil, they will not raise the price of heating fuel and gasoline.

Captain Squint, who was at the wheel, angrily said, "That's a hell of a place to put a lighthouse!"

ALI IN MOON SHOT?

MUHAMMED ALI TO ATTEMPT COMEBACK

"The Greatest" on comeback trail

CHICAGO—Former heavyweight champion, Muhammad Ali, announced today that he will try to regain the heavyweight championship one more time. The ex-champ said he doesn't need the money, he is fighting because the fans deserve to see the "greatest fighter of all time" in action once again.

Promoter Donald King says this will be the first billion dollar gate in history and he is planning to hold the bout in Ohio. When asked "where" in Ohio, King replied, "The whole state! Man, I'm talking tickets!"

FUTURE
NOSTALGIA

A Nostalgic Look at the Movies of the '70's

THAT'S ENTERTAINMENT III

Singing in the rain . . ., I'm singing in the rain . . . Hi, I'm Gene Kelly! I'm going to be your guide as we take a look at some of the great movie musicals of the '70's . . .
Hold It!

One of my favorite war movies, "The DIRTIEST DOZEN", was shot right here! It began with a brutal hanging and ended with people being burned alive! And the cast was a dream . . . Borgnine was a psychotic general . . . Donald Sutherland a degenerate rapist . . . Jimmy Brown a blood thirsty killer . . . Telly Savalas a criminally insane murderer . . . Lee Marvin a sadistic officer . . . and I was the **good** guy, a **normal** murderer!

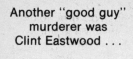

Another "good guy" murderer was Clint Eastwood . . .

Bronson, of all your movies, the one I enjoyed the most was when you portrayed an architect who decided to do something about changing the New York scene . . .

Yeah, I enjoyed playing that dedicated police officer! But I'll always be grateful to those spaghetti westerns which allowed me the artistic freedom to express myself as a killer, like "A FISTFUL OF GUTS."

Who are they, a couple of angry commuters?

For the last time, Senora, what time ees the stage arriving?

No, gringo, they are banditos. The lady's husband ees the stagecoach driver and he ees breenging een a shipment of gold.

Gold?

Another bloody biggie that had them screaming in the aisles was "JAWZ."

Like when I played "SLAUGHTERER" . . .

Sorry, I must be in the wrong place, I was looking for the Police Station.

This **is** the police station.

What happened?

Somebody called him, 'boy'.

One white film that really turned me on was that teenaged flick GORRIE

And who will ever forget the Oscar winning car chase in THE FRENCH MISCONNECTION?

Yeah, that was a great film. Another kind of movie we enjoyed were the disaster films like EARTHQUAKER . . .

No revue of the films of the '70's would be complete without some mention of the KUNG FU movies! These were true art films! All the unnecessary frills like plot and dialogue were eliminated, leaving nothing but pure violence . . .

All of these terrific movies owe
a debt of gratitude to those
fabulous pioneers of screen violence,
the immortal Three Stooges . . .

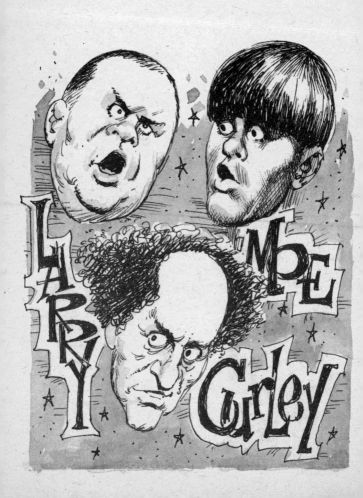

FUTURE PERSONALIZED CHECKS

The trend toward "tell it like it is" realism will result in personalized checks that will reflect the true picture of the person himself . . .

WHAT THEY LOOK LIKE TODAY:

Arnold Furd
29 Ivy Tower Drive
Los Angeles, California

PAY TO THE
ORDER OF MATT'S BOOK STORE $ 23.89

TWENTY THREE AND 89/100 ———— DOLLARS

NATIONAL
CATASTROPHE
& LOAN

Arnold Furd

COLLEGE STUDENT

WHAT THEY WILL LOOK LIKE IN THE FUTURE:

Arnold Furd
29 Ivy Tower Drive
Los Angeles, California

PAY TO THE
ORDER OF CASH $ 100.00

ONE HUNDRED AND 00/00 DOLLARS

NATIONAL
CATASTROPHE
& LOAN

Arnold Furd

WHAT THEY LOOK LIKE TODAY:

Hon. Matthew R. Beane
897 Justice Blvd.
Great Neck, New York

PAY TO THE
ORDER OF J. D. ROBB CLEANERS $ 75.00

Seventy five and 00 ——— DOLLARS

NATIONAL
CATASTROPHE
& LOAN

Matthew R. Beane

JUDGE

WHAT THEY WILL LOOK LIKE IN THE FUTURE:

Hon. Matthew R. Beane
897 Justice Blvd.
Great Neck, New York

PAY TO THE
ORDER OF Cash $ 2,000.—

Two thousand and 00 ——— DOLLARS

NATIONAL
CATASTROPHE
& LOAN

Matthew R. Beane

WHAT THEY LOOK LIKE TODAY:

Mack Macho
32 Special St.
Twin Falls, Minnesota

PAY TO THE
ORDER OF _Ammo-RAMA_ $ 211 53/100

Two hundred & Eleven 53/100 DOLLARS

NATIONAL
CATASTROPHE
& LOAN

Mack Macho

OUTDOORSMAN

WHAT THEY WILL LOOK LIKE IN THE FUTURE:

Mack Macho
32 Special St.
Twin Falls, Minnesota

PAY TO THE
ORDER OF _N.R.A._ $ 25 00/100

Twenty-five and DOLLARS

NATIONAL
CATASTROPHE
& LOAN

Mack Macho

WHAT THEY LOOK LIKE TODAY:

Gen. Bruce Boondock
Headquarters
Fort Sumter, South Carolina

PAY TO THE
ORDER OF *God & Country Society* $ 15.00

Fifteen ————————— DOLLARS

NATIONAL
CATASTROPHE
& LOAN

Gen. Bruce Boondock

ARMY GENERAL

WHAT THEY WILL LOOK LIKE IN THE FUTURE:

Gen. Bruce Boondock
Headquarters
Fort Sumter, South Carolina

PAY TO THE
ORDER OF *God & Country Society* $ 15.00

Fifteen ————————— DOLLARS

NATIONAL
CATASTROPHE
& LOAN

Gen. Bruce Boondock

WHAT THEY LOOK LIKE TODAY:

Jacques Stroppe
13 Shmickle Way
Dallas, Texas

PAY TO THE
ORDER OF _Vitamin Village_ $ 13.45

thirteen 45/XX _____ DOLLARS

NATIONAL
CATASTROPHE
& LOAN   _Jacques Stroppe_

FOOTBALL PLAYER

WHAT THEY WILL LOOK LIKE IN THE FUTURE:

Jacques Stroppe
13 Shmickle Way
Dallas, Texas

PAY TO THE
ORDER OF _CASH_ $ 200.00

two hundred 00/XX _____ DOLLARS

NATIONAL
CATASTROPHE
& LOAN   _Jacques Stroppe_

FUTURE XMAS SPECIALS

The characters will be the same, but they will be a lot more "real" than they are today— like, for instance . . .

RUDOLPH REDNOSE
The Reindeer

Once upon a time there was a Reindeer named Rudolph. He lived in the North Pole at Santa's Toyland. . .

Rudolph was a good Reindeer and he always obeyed his parents. But he was different from the other Reindeer—had a large red nose that glowed in the dark!

One day, Santa announced tryouts for his sled team. . .

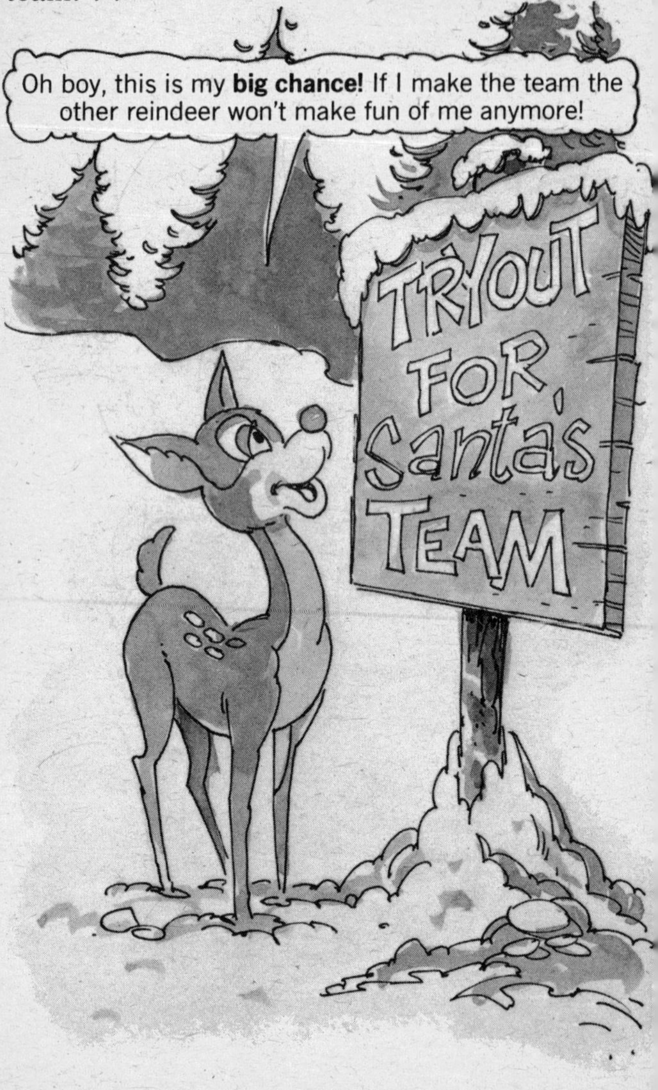

Rudolph tried hard to make the team. He ran as fast as he could, won the windsprings, and he jumped higher than the other deer. . .

Then Xmas Eve arrived, it was a dark, stormy night and the fog as thick as chocolate syrup. . .

Many of the familiar species of marine, animal and plant life are being threatened with extinction by the emergence of deadly man made creatures. These new specimens are all around us. Just look out your window and you'll be amazed at how many you see. In order to help you properly identify these creatures, here is . . .

MODERN WILDLIFE SPECIES

THE THROWAWAY BOTTLE
NO DEPOSITUS

This rapidly growing species comes in various sizes and can be identified by the colorful marlings on its' plumage. Some of the more common specimens read Pepsi, Coke, 7UP, Schlitz, Ballantine. Throw away bottles are considered dangerous, especially when thrown from a moving car or when broken. They are usually seen in large numbers after a group of high school kids have a beer bust or a beach party.

THE FLAVORLESS CHEWING GUM GLOB
STICKUM DISGUSTUS

Huge flocks of this small specimen may be encountered on any sidewalk in the USA, but their favorite roosting place is inside of theatres. They may be found on the underside of the chair arm, seat or on the floor. You'll know when you sit on or step on 'Flavorless Chewing Gum Glob' as you will be stuck to the seat or the floor. These are leech like creatures and once they attach themselves to your shoes or pants they stay forever.

THE GREAT BLACK OIL SLICK
SLIMUS SPILLUM

This huge creature is becoming a familiar sight at many beaches and waterways. They are extremely harmful to all forms of life, marine, fowl and human. They usually appear when a cheaply made, rusty oil tanker splits apart or when an oil company that is drilling in the ocean has an accident. The Great Black Oil Slick grows rapidly and is often several miles in size. Since the oil companies are responsible for these creatures, what efforts are they making to combat it? They are spending millions of dollars hiring celebrities to do commercials telling us what a great job the oil companies are doing.

THE SPOTTED FAST FOOD CONTAINER
BIGUS MACKUS

A relatively new species, the Spotted Fast Food Container, is multiplying at an alarming rate. They can be seen in school yards, parks, sidewalks, along the highways and are found both in the cities and in the rural areas. They are usually white in color and their plumage is spotted with grease stains, red ketchup smears and other yecchy stuff. Originally a native American, this creature has migrated and has been sighted in large numbers as far away as Japan. It is rumored to have been seen on the moon following the American landing.

THE COMMON BEER CAN
ALUMINUS FLIPTOPUS

The Common Beer Can and his close cousin, the Common Soda Can, congregate in large numbers in parking lots, under grandstands at high school athletic events and are also found on beaches and along the highway. They are easily recognizable at night by their reflective quality.

Though harmless in appearance, they can inflict damage to tires. They are usually cylindrical in shape but many species are bent and crushed as it is considered macho in some circles to squeeze these creatures out of shape after drinking their contents.

THE RUSTY ABANDONED CAR
HUNKUS JUNKUS

The natural habitat of this unsightly beast is usually a side street in a major city. These large creatures have strange molting habits; as soon as they are nested down they start shedding. First their wheels, batteries and meters disappear, their windows become mysteriously smashed and their seats vanish. Soon there is nothing left but a big dented, rusting shell. Once a Rusty Abandoned Car settles in your neighbourhood, he will not move unless towed away.

THE LONG NECKED BELCHING SMOKESTACK
THICKUS SMOGUS

This large unsightly species can be found in any large city. It is easily recognized by the black smoke, soot and other gook it spits out into the air. These creatures are truly remarkable and can block out the sun with their smoke. They are a major health hazard to all forms of life and cause millions of dollars in pollution damage every year. The Longed Neck Belching Smokestack can be controlled by placing filter traps over their mouths to trap the pollutants. This process is felt to be too costly and would cut into corporation profits and this is considered Un-American. Polluting the air is the American Way.

THE DRIED OUT XMAS TREE
TANNEBAUM THROWOUTUS

This strange creature appears every year at the same time, a week after Xmas. It has a shiny green coat and often has pieces of bright silver tinsel clinging to it. A few days after they settle down, their needles begin to fall out and their green coat turns to a dull brown color. They eventually disappear but you can be sure that next year after Xmas the Dried Out Xmas Tree will show up in front of your house. They are usually bearers of sad tidings because their appearance signals the end of vacation and the return to school.

Back in the early days of psychiatry, shrinks were asked to treat normal, every day disorders like schizophrenia, paranoia, and flashing! But as the world progressed and life became more complex, so did neuroses. To help keep shrinks abreast of the latest in psychological information, research institutes and medical centers issue *bulletins*! These bulletins assist them in recognizing and treating the newest and kinkiest mental disorders, most of them, they've discovered, the result of TV addiction . . .

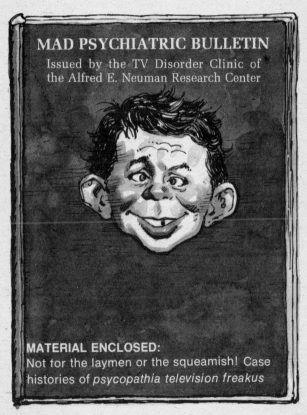

MAD PSYCHIATRIC BULLETIN

Issued by the TV Disorder Clinic of the Alfred E. Neuman Research Center

MATERIAL ENCLOSED:
Not for the laymen or the squeamish! Case histories of *psycopathia television freakus*

CASE HISTORY #5: *Toilet Paper Addict*

CAROL C.—*Housewife, married*

Mrs. C engaged in average, typical housewife activities; talking on the phone, watching soap operas, shopping and talking on the phone about soap operas and shopping. While at the supermarket one day, Mrs. C. was seized with an uncontrollable urge to squeeze a package of toilet paper. After this first encounter, Mrs. C. was "hooked," ignoring her TV set, telephone, children, and her husband Stanley, although Stanley hadn't noticed any difference in his wife's behavior, having been ignored for years. Crisis stage was reached when Mrs. C. was banned from the supermarket by the effeminate department manager who had received numerous complaints from customers who refused to purchase already-squeezed packages. Her supply source thus dried up, Mrs. C. hid her cabinet supply from other members of the household, forcing them great inconvenience and discomfort. Finally, at the urging of her minister, Mrs. C. agreed to seek psychiatric help. *Her analyst reports:* "Mrs. C. is coming along. However, Stanley C., her husband, appears to be beyond help, having suffered the ultimate rejection by his wife's actions. His last words before entering a catatonic state was 'Another man I could understand, but a roll of toilet paper?' "

CASE HISTORY #19 *Collar Voyeur*

HULGA R.—*Train conductor, divorced*

Ms. R. was the first female conductor appointed to the Atchison, Topeka and Johnny Mercer Railroad, showing no early signs of psychological disorder by this radical change from her former housewife role. The first reported incident took place on the 7:42 Commuter Special. Punching a passenger's monthly ticket, Ms. R. looked at the man's collar and began shouting, "Ring around the collar!" Several passengers who had been engrossed in their magazines, got off the speeding train, believing she was calling their stop. Legal suits are still pending. The condition grew progressively worse, Ms. R. screaming "Ring around the collar!" to more than half the passengers riding her train cars. This, together with the fact that her concentration on shirt collars often resulted in her punching holes in neckties and lapels instead of tickets, caused Ms. R. to be fired. A nationwide strike was threatened by the union if Ms. R.'s firing was enforced, however, so Hulga reluctantly returned to her job. Union medical benefits included psychological treatment, and Ms. R. took advantage of this. *Her analyst reports:* "Ms. R. will only respond to treatment if I am dressed in white from head to toe and call myself "the man from Glad." Her color fixation is the direct result of her appointment to the railroad service. The trauma was not that she was the first woman appointed, but the first white person to gain employment in this capacity!"

CASE HISTORY #23: *Blindfold Beer-Drinking Syndrome*

MURRAY T.—*Artist, married*

Murray T. has been a successful illustrator for 18 years. After a hard day at the drawing board, he would often join other free lance friends at a local tavern and partake of a bottle of beer or two and stimulating conversation. One particular day he engaged in a friendly wager with a friend, putting on a blindfold and comparing two different brands of beer. Murray T. soon found he couldn't enjoy beer *without* a blindfold, even in the privacy of his own home. This caused a sudden drop in his income, as he could neither stop the blindfold beer drinking nor carry out his drawing assignments with his eyes covered, (although some of his peers believed he was doing better work in this fashion). His wife threatened to leave him unless he sought psychiatric help. *His analyst reports:* I am the second analyst that has seen Mr. T. in relation to his problem. The first, Dr. Porges P., in a daring, unprecedented experiment sought to prove to Mr. T. that a blindfold didn't affect the taste of beer. The experiment did not prove constructive, as Dr. P. soon became a blindfold beer addict himself. They can be seen any evening blindfolded, drinking beer together and laughingly declaring they would "shrink every head off every glass of beer in town!" Mr. T. may eventually come out of his present state. Less hope is given Dr. P., whose CASE HISTORY #87 is currently being prepared."

CASE HISTORY #34: *Paper Towel Deviate*

SUSAN H.—*Airline stewardess, unmarried*

As is demanded from most stewardesses, Ms. H.'s is expected to look sexy and clean up spilled drinks (resulting from her looking sexy), dropped food, and leaky barf bags (many wives get upset over sexy stewardesses). Ms. H. used paper towels to perform her clean-up duties, finding after prolonged use, that paper towels became a turn-on. In order to use them more often, Ms. H. began spilling things "accidently," and found she could also experience a high by stuffing paper towels in water and watching them absorb, or balancing full cups of coffee on wet paper towels. She performed some of these activities instead of her other in-flight duties while hiding in the john. This strategey failed to go unnoticed, as 747 tourist class john facilities are inadequate to begin with, and Ms. H. was canned for too much time in the can. Ms. H. is currently being treated at the Cuckoo Nest, a rest home she frequently flew over while a stewardess. *Her analyst reports:* "The patient is improving steadily, responding to our "slow down" withdrawal procedures which enable her to forsake paper towel sopping for toilet paper squeezing (see CASE HISTORY #5)"

A FUTURE UFO LANDING

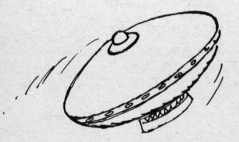

What will emerge?

Where did it come from?

IT CAME FROM THE PLANET ZUCCHINI!

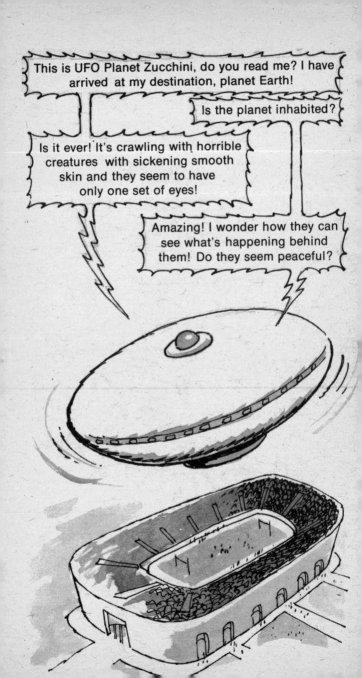

I'm Lt. Koomish! I'd like to ask you folks a few questions! Was there anything unusual about the perpetrator?
Well—he was bigger than a linebacker, taller than a basketball player, and he had Four eyes!
Would you two mind coming down and looking through our mug file?

There's nothing here, Lt., except these . . .
Hmm, they look like oversized **prune pits!**
That's it! The creature looked like a gigantic prune!
This might be serious! I'm going to advise the Mayor of what has transpired! Meanwhile, you men look around and see what you can come up with!

Hello, I'm Dr. Zelda Mulch and this is Gen. Boondock! If we may, we'd like to ask you some questions . . .
Be my guest! My name is Prunus! My rank is Ltd.! And my serial number is All-Bran 155!
Okay, Mac, where are you from, Moscow or Peking?

You don't understand, we reproduce by planting seeds in the **soil!** Unfortunately, on Zucchini you can't excavate more than six inches down without striking **oil!**
OIL? Oil?
That's correct! Our planet is inundated with oil, useless, yecchy oil!

And just suppose this creature reveals the secret of harnessing the sun's energy? It would destroy our God-given American way of life!

Zelda, I'd like to, believe me! But I have a job to do! I've got to find a fertile planet to plant my seeds! Besides, there isn't enough room on the space ship! But I'll always remember you as a **friend . . .**
A friend? Man or Prune, you're all alike!
I'm sorry . . . you were really a **peach . . .**
I guess, coming from you that's an improvement! Thanks . . .

THE END ?